"It's a bad idea," Junior mumbled.

"What are you talking about?" Teddy asked.

"You guys won't like it if my dad sponsors the team, believe me," Junior said quietly. "And then you'll blame *me*."

"Blame you for what?" Felipe called. He hurried over to us.

"You don't know how my dad is about hockey!" Junior said. "He talks about it all the time. We have three television sets so he can watch three games at once. Every morning he reads the hockey news before anything else. We go to Chicago twice a month to see the Blackhawks play."

"Cool," Felipe said. "Does he really watch three games at once? Wow."

"We think Ron should ask his dad to be our sponsor," I told Felipe. "He owns a business in West Monroeville."

"You don't understand," Junior repeated. "It's a bad idea. Take my word for it."

"Look, Ron," Teddy said. "No matter

what happens, we won't blame you. I promise. We just want to play hockey."

"Yeah," Felipe said. "Ted's right. We have to play. *Please* ask your dad."

Junior was silent for a minute. "Okay," he finally whispered. "You asked for it."

The No Stars need all the fans they can get! So don't miss:

#1 STICKING IT OUT

#2 THE PUCK STOPS HERE!

#3 CALL ME GRETZKY!

#4 LET'S HEAR IT FOR THE SHRUMPS!

4

LET'S HEAR IT FOR THE SHRUMPS!

By Jim O'Connor

●

Bullseye Books

Random House 🏠 **New York**

The No Stars™ are created by
Parachute Press, Inc.

Ice hockey equipment provided by ⬥CANSTAR
Sports, Inc., makers of *Bauer* and *Cooper*
hockey equipment and ice skates.

A BULLSEYE BOOK PUBLISHED BY RANDOM HOUSE, INC.
Copyright © 1996 by Parachute Press, Inc.
All rights reserved under International and Pan-American Copyright
Conventions. Published in the United States by Random House, Inc.,
New York, and simultaneously in Canada by Random House of Canada
Limited, Toronto.
http://www.randomhouse.com/

Library of Congress Catalog Card Number: 95-73062
ISBN: 0-679-87909-9
RL: 2.1

Printed in the United States of America 10 9 8 7 6 5 4 3 2 1

THE NO STARS is a trademark of Parachute Press, Inc.

CONTENTS

CONTENTS

Good-bye, Spiro

1

"We're on a roll, Mike," Teddy Ryan called to me. "Our rotten luck has *finally* changed."

Our hockey team, the No Stars, had just finished practicing. Teddy and I were skating around the rink to cool off.

"What are you talking about?" I asked Teddy. "We've won exactly one game."

Teddy's my best friend, but sometimes he doesn't make any sense. Like right now. I mean, our team is terrible. That's why everyone calls us the No Stars instead of our real name—the North Stars.

"Right!" Teddy answered. "And remember who we beat. The *Sharks*. The best team in the Eastside League."

"So what?" I said. "Nothing has really changed. We have the same guys. Everyone *looks* the same. Everyone skates the same. You make it sound like we suddenly turned into the New York Rangers. Beating the Sharks was just a lucky break."

"Come on, Mike. Think about our practice tonight. Nobody goofed up. Not once!"

Some of the other No Stars stood by the goal at the far end of the rink. They passed a puck around. Teddy pointed his stick at them.

"Cliff didn't fall down once tonight. Lucas didn't lose his temper. Sari didn't complain about anything. We're playing like a real team. You know I'm right," Teddy said.

"Yeah, when you put it that way," I said. "But..."

"But what?"

"Well, even if we did beat the Sharks, suppose it was just luck? Maybe we won't win another game."

"No way," Teddy replied. "I tell you, we're going to win a *lot* more games. We've had all the bad luck any team can have. What else could possibly go wrong?"

"I hope you're right!" I smiled at him as we skated over to our team bench.

"Hey, guys, looking good," Ronald Shrump, Jr., yelled to us. "Mike, you had two goals and three assists tonight. And Teddy, you had a goal and five assists!"

"Big deal," I said. "This was a *practice*, not a game. Anyone can score goals when they're not being checked."

Ronald gets on our nerves, and that's

why we call him Junior. When his friend Wayne "Wild Man" Wilder became the No Stars' new goalie, Junior started tagging along to all our practices and games. He's here all the time. I don't get it. He doesn't even play hockey.

But he doesn't just sit and watch us play either. Not Junior. Junior talks. And talks. He never shuts up!

"Hey, guys! Nice work. Hey, guys! Great goal. Hey, guys...hey, guys...hey, guys!" All the time.

Or he asks stupid hockey trivia questions. Not stuff like "Who scored the most goals in the NHL last year?" Or "Who won the Stanley Cup in 1963?"

Junior asks you what size skate Wayne Gretzky wears. Or how many players in the National Hockey League have black dogs named Midnight. All sorts of crazy stuff.

Now, I love hockey, but give me a break!

It's hard to play a good game when you feel as if you're on one of those TV trivia shows!

Then last week, Junior appointed himself our unofficial team manager. He got even worse.

"Hey, guys, don't forget to lace up your skates! Hey, Mike, don't forget your stick." He was everywhere!

Tonight Junior had two whistles and a stopwatch draped around his neck. He had a water bottle stuck in his hip pocket. He carried a clipboard.

"What's that?" Teddy asked Junior, pointing at his arm.

"Tissues," Junior explained. "In case anyone has to blow their nose. Always be prepared, I say!"

A little package of tissues was taped to his arm.

"You're too much, Junior," I said. "Come on, Teddy. Let's get going."

"Okay, guys," Junior shouted. "Don't forget. Practice is at six A.M. *sharp* on Saturday."

"Right, Junior," Teddy muttered.

"Is he driving you crazy, too?" I whispered to Teddy while we changed out of our skates.

"Totally," Teddy said. "He must say 'Hey, guys' every five seconds. That's all I hear on the ice. I even hear it in my sleep! He's making everyone nuts."

"I know what you mean," I said. "Do you think we could talk to the Wild Man about Junior? Maybe he can get rid of him."

"Are you kidding?" Teddy said. "Junior is Wild Man's best friend!" He pulled his hockey helmet off and stuffed it into his equipment bag. He pushed one hand through his long, straight brown hair and then put on his glasses. He wears them all the time, except when he's skating.

"Well, we've got to do *something* about Junior," I said. "Call me after dinner. Maybe we can think up a plan."

"Okay," Teddy said.

We walked out of the rink together. Teddy's mom was waiting in her car. They live on the other side of town, so Teddy can't walk home from practice the way I do.

Felipe Perez and Lucas Wilson waved to me from the sidewalk in front of the rink. We live near each other and usually walk home together. We started down Taylor Street toward the center of town.

If you live in Monroeville, Wisconsin, you have to love hockey. Everyone plays it all winter long. And all summer long, too. Hockey rules in Monroeville.

"Hey, guys!" Felipe said. "Nice practice. Hey, Mike, nice pass. Hey, Lucas, great shot."

"What—?" I began. Then I smiled. I got

it. Felipe had made his voice high and squeaky like Junior's.

"Sari, you hit the puck left-handed seven times and right-handed six times," I said, pretending to be Junior, too. "Felipe, you bounced it off your head twice!"

Then Lucas started in. "Hey, guys! Do you know how many New Jersey Devils eat bologna sandwiches for breakfast?" Lucas's parents are getting divorced, and he doesn't joke around much anymore. I was glad to see him laughing.

"Pass me a tissue," I yelled.

"Ask Junior," Felipe teased. "He's always prepared!"

Lucas pretended to blow his nose on his shirt.

By the time we reached the corner of Taylor and West Wisconsin Avenue, we were all screaming and laughing about Junior.

"Hey, guys!" Felipe cried. "Whoa! I

don't believe this..." He stopped and pointed across the street.

I turned and looked. Spiro's Diner, the best place in Monroeville for greasy French fries and extra-thick chocolate shakes, was dark and closed.

"What happened?" I asked. "Do you think they had a fire or something?"

"There's a sign on the door," Lucas said.

We ran across the street and over to Spiro's front door. The sign said, CLOSED BY THE BOARD OF HEALTH.

And underneath the sign, a sheet of paper was taped to the inside of the glass door. It said, OUT OF BUSINESS. GOOD-BYE. SPIRO.

None of us said anything for a minute. We all loved Spiro's. I sure would miss those French fries.

But Spiro's was also our team sponsor. The No Stars' full name is really "The

Spiro's Diner North Stars." Every team has a sponsor—the Earl's Pharmacy Penguins, the Wisconsin Electric Red Wings, the Quik Tred Islanders.

"I don't believe it!" Felipe cried. "Do you know what this means?"

"Yeah," I answered. "It means the No Stars are in trouble again!"

"I don't get it," Lucas said. "What are you guys talking about? What's the big deal?"

"If Spiro's is out of business, we don't have a sponsor," I explained. "And that means we can't play hockey!"

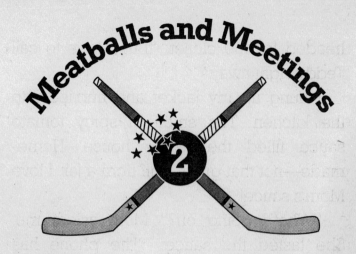

Meatballs and Meetings

2

"I'm home, Mom!" I shouted as I walked in the front door. "I have to call Teddy right away. You won't believe what happened!"

I pulled my North Stars team jacket off and threw it on the big overstuffed chair. My dog, Ranger, ran into the living room and licked my face.

"Michael Beagleman! How many times do I have to tell you to hang up your coat?" Mom called from the kitchen.

"Sorry," I said. I patted Ranger for a second, then picked up my jacket and headed for the closet. "But I *have* to call Teddy right away."

I hung up my jacket and hurried into the kitchen. The smell of spicy tomato sauce filled the whole house. Home-made—not that gross stuff from a jar. I love Mom's sauce!

"What's going on?" Mom asked me. She tasted the sauce. "The phone has been ringing off the hook. First Sari called you. Then Teddy. Then Brendan. And Sari called again a couple of minutes ago. There's going to be a team meeting at her house tonight. Something about Spiro's."

"I guess I don't have to call Teddy," I said. "How did they all find out so fast?"

"Find out what?" Mom stirred some salt into the sauce and covered it.

"Spiro's Diner was closed by the Board of Health," I explained. "We have to get a new sponsor right away. Or we can't play."

"Wow, that's bad news," Mom said. "But

are you sure Spiro's is really closed for good?"

"Yeah," I answered. "There's a sign that says, 'Out of Business.' I guess this meeting is about getting a new sponsor for the team."

"Well, I'd better let you eat dinner early," Mom said. "Dad has a meeting at school tonight, and he'll be home late. I'll drive you over to Sari's after you eat."

My dad teaches history at the high school. He comes to all the No Stars' games and rings a cowbell when we score. *If* we score!

"I can't believe our rotten luck this year," I said. "First we lost our coach when Mr. Slocum broke his leg, and we had to find a new one. Then Steve Slocum quit, and we had to find a new goalie."

I opened the refrigerator and poured myself a glass of milk.

"Just remember how all those 'disasters' turned out," Mom said. "Sari's mom is a terrific coach. And little Wayne is the best goalie the No Stars have ever had."

I sat down at the table and took a sip of milk.

Mom kept talking as she finished making my dinner. "Plus, who scored the winning goal when the No Stars beat the Sharks? You did! So cheer up!" Mom set a big bowl of spaghetti and meatballs down in front of me.

I nodded. My mom always finds a way to make things seem okay. I picked up my fork and twirled it in the spaghetti. Ranger sat under the table. I secretly knocked one meatball out of my bowl. It fell under the table. Ranger gobbled it and wagged her tail.

"Mike, don't feed the dog," Mom scolded.

"Who, me?" I asked with a big smile.

Most of the team was already at Sari's

house when Mom dropped me off after dinner. Brendan Murphy, Randy Fernandez, and Tommy Feldman were squeezed together on the couch. Teddy and Peter Lomenzo were sprawled on the floor in front of the television set. Cliff Parkes, our biggest and tallest player, sat in Mr. Baxter's leather lounge chair. He had a bowl of popcorn in his lap.

Felipe, Sari, and her mom, whom we call "Coach B.," stood by the kitchen door. The rest of the guys sat on the floor all around the room.

"Hi, Mike," Coach B. called. "Find an empty spot and sit down."

She turned to Felipe. "I think the team captain should lead the meeting, don't you?"

Felipe smiled and stood straighter. He takes being captain of the No Stars very seriously.

"All right, guys, here's the story," Felipe

began. "My dad called Spiro. He *definitely* isn't going to reopen the diner. He's moving to Florida."

"Why did the Board of Health close it down?" I asked. "A little grease never hurt anyone."

"Excuse me! Hey, guys, coming through. Sorry we're late!" Junior and Wayne pushed past everyone and sat down in the middle of the floor.

"Oh, great," I muttered.

"Hey, guys, what's going down?" Junior asked. He pushed his dark hair away from his glasses.

Felipe took a deep breath. "I don't know why the Board of Health closed Spiro's," he said. "The main thing is, we have to find a new sponsor right away. We have to figure out what we're going to do."

Felipe looked around the room. "Do any of you guys know someone who would sponsor us?" he asked hopefully.

We stared at one another. No one said a word. I tried to think of a good idea. Any idea. Nothing came to me.

"How about your parents?" Coach B. asked us. "Does anyone's mom or dad own a store?"

We all shook our heads.

"Well, I have a plan then," Coach B. said. She stepped into the room.

"Tomorrow afternoon, we're going to meet again. This time, in front of Spiro's. The whole team is going to walk around town and visit every store. We'll ask every store owner if he or she wants to be our sponsor. I've split the team into four groups. That way we can visit a lot of stores in one afternoon."

She picked up her clipboard and started reading off names. "Teddy, Sari, and Brendan will cover the west side of Main Street. Tommy, Randy, and Cliff will do the east side. Lucas, Tony, and Peter will visit all the stores on West Wisconsin Avenue. Felipe, Mike, and Wayne will check out Taylor Street—"

"What about me, Coach? Who do I go with?" Junior shouted. He waved his hand right in her face.

"Ronald. Thanks for helping us," Coach B. said. "Why don't you go with Wayne and...Felipe and Mike. Okay, guys?"

I looked at Felipe and he looked at me. I knew he was thinking the same thing I was. Now was the time to get rid of Junior once and for all. We would just say, "No way!"

"Sure, Coach," Felipe blurted out. "He can come with me and Mike. Right, Mike?"

Mrs. B. turned to me with a smile on her face.

How could Felipe have chickened out like that? What was I supposed to do now?

If I said "No way" all by myself, I'd look like the biggest jerk.

"Sure. Junior can come with us," I mumbled.

I had no choice. Junior was here to stay—at least for today.

Junior's Secret

The next day after school, we met in front of Spiro's. Coach B. handed each of us a sheet of paper with a speech printed on it.

It said:

"Hi, my name is (say your name) and I play hockey for the Westside North Stars. We're looking for a new sponsor for our team. Sponsoring a youth hockey team is a great way to help the young men and women of Monroeville. If you are interested in sponsoring us, please sign the attached form. An official of the Monroeville West-

side *Hockey League will contact you."*

"This is just a guide," Coach B. said. "You don't have to read it word for word. But make sure you cover the important points. Okay. Is everybody here?"

"Wayne can't make it, Coach," Junior said. "He has a virus. The school nurse sent him home after lunch."

"Thank you, Ronald," Coach B. said. "That means it's just you, Felipe, and Mike. Why don't you guys get started?"

"Oh, great," I whispered to Felipe. "Junior is going to drive me crazy. I was counting on Wayne to keep him away from us."

"Let's go," Felipe said to Junior.

"And get this over with," I muttered under my breath.

My dad always says that you shouldn't judge people until you get to know them. Sometimes you can be all wrong about a person. Like Sari, for instance. The first day she joined the No Stars, I was sure I wouldn't like her. She turned out to be really cool, though.

But Junior...well, he ended up being as annoying as I thought he would be. Like when we went into Roberts's Shoe Repair. Mr. Roberts was arranging cans of shoe polish on a shelf.

"Good afternoon, Mr. Roberts," Felipe said. "My name is Felipe Perez, and I play for the Westside North Stars hockey team—"

"Except that we're called the No Stars," Junior interrupted. "Because we're not very good. Right now we're only scoring 2.4 goals per game. And our defense is letting the other teams score an average of 5.9 goals per game..."

Mr. Roberts put down the cans of polish and stared at Junior.

"Will you cool it?" I whispered in Junior's ear. I nudged him with my elbow.

"I'm telling him about the No Stars," he answered.

"*North* Stars! Junior, we're the North Stars," I whispered. "Do you want to scare him off completely? He'll never sponsor a team that sounds like a bunch of losers."

I looked up. Now Mr. Roberts was staring at me and shaking his head. He held open the door.

"Maybe next year, guys," he said. He shut the door behind us.

"Well, that didn't go so badly," Junior said. "You heard him say he might sponsor us next year."

"Great, Junior. Just great," I said. "We need a sponsor *this year*. We need one *now!*"

Junior didn't say anything for almost a whole minute. It was the longest I'd ever heard him be quiet.

"Ah, Mike, could you do me a favor?" he said.

"What?"

"Well, I really don't like being called Junior. All my friends call me Ron."

"We're not friends," I said.

"Oh," Junior mumbled. I felt bad. I didn't want to be mean to Junior, but sometimes he made me so angry.

We visited five more stores and didn't have any luck finding a sponsor. We came really close once.

Mrs. Bascomb, the manager of the Monroeville Twoplex Cinema, was in her office. After Felipe gave his speech, she smiled. "I love hockey. I'd be happy to sign the form."

Felipe handed it to her, and she reached for a pen.

"I see you have a Montreal Canadiens banner," Junior said. He pointed to the red-and-white banner hanging on the office wall.

"That's right," Mrs. Bascomb said. "I've

been a Canadiens fan since I was your age." She glanced down at the form.

"Too bad they lose more than they win these days," Junior went on. "It's hard to believe they can play so badly—"

Mrs. Bascomb put her pen down and handed the form back to Felipe. The form was still empty. No sponsor. Two minutes later, we were standing on the sidewalk in front of the theater.

We met up with the rest of the team near the police station. None of them had found a sponsor either.

"What are we going to do?" Sari asked her mom.

"We'll find someone, Sari. I'm sure of it," Coach B. answered. But she didn't look so sure to me.

"Hey, guys! There's my dad," Junior said. He pointed down the street to a big black Jeep. "He must have left his store early."

I shot a quick look at Teddy. Teddy raised his eyebrows at me. "Store?" we said.

"I've got to go," Junior said, but Teddy grabbed his arm.

"What kind of store?" I asked.

"It's a business. Not a real store. Honest," Junior said. "It's over in West Monroeville. On a back road. Nobody ever goes there."

I glanced down the street at Mr. Shrump. Then at Junior. Junior suddenly looked pale and nervous. Real nervous. Something was fishy.

"Let go of him," I told Teddy. "Hey, Ron, do you think your dad's store could sponsor us?"

"It's not a store!" Junior sprinted over to the Jeep. Teddy and I raced after him.

"Dad, this is Mike and Teddy. They're both on the team," Junior said as we both stood by the curb, panting.

"Hi, guys!" Mr. Shrump said in a booming voice. "I've heard a lot about the North Stars. Or should I say No Stars? You guys are having quite a season. Did Ron tell you I used to be a hockey player myself?"

Mr. Shrump was just like Junior. He talked and talked and talked. Mainly about hockey. You could tell that Junior had heard it all before. Sometimes he would finish a sentence for his dad.

"Yeah," Mr. Shrump said. "The greatest defenseman in the history of hockey is—?"

"Bobby Orr," Junior finished.

"Excuse us for a minute, Mr. Shrump," I said. "Teddy and I have to ask Jun—I mean Ron—something."

I grabbed Junior by the arm and walked him away from his dad.

Teddy followed us.

"Ron," I said. "Why don't you get your dad to sponsor us? It would be great for the team if someone's parent was our sponsor. Good for your dad's business, too. The sponsor doesn't have to be a store."

Junior didn't say anything. He just stared at the ground.

"Well, how about it?" I asked. "Your dad's got his own business, right? He's not sponsoring another team, right? He loves hockey, right?"

Junior shook his head. "No. I can't do it. Sorry, but I just can't."

"Why not?" Teddy asked him.

"It's a secret."

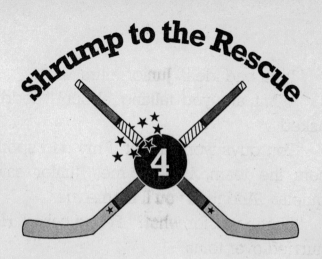

Shrump to the Rescue

4

"**W**hy won't you ask him?" Teddy asked Junior. "I bet he would say 'yes.' Your dad loves hockey."

Junior shook his head. "No! You just don't understand."

"Come on...Ron," I said. "You have to! Your dad's our last chance!"

Junior folded his arms across his chest and stared at the ground.

"Give me one good reason why you won't ask him," Teddy demanded.

That's what I like about Teddy. When he wants something, he doesn't give up.

"It's a bad idea," Junior mumbled.

"What are you talking about?" Teddy asked.

"You guys won't like it if my dad sponsors the team, believe me," Junior said quietly. "And then you'll blame *me*."

"Blame you for what?" Felipe called. He hurried over to us.

"You don't know how my dad is about hockey!" Junior said. "He talks about it all the time. We have three television sets so he can watch three games at once. Every morning he reads the hockey news before anything else. We go to Chicago twice a month to see the Blackhawks play."

"Cool," Felipe said. "Does he really watch three games at once? Wow."

"We think Ron should ask his dad to be our sponsor," I told Felipe. "He owns a business in West Monroeville."

"You don't understand," Junior repeated. "It's a bad idea. Take my word for it."

"Look, Ron," Teddy said. "No matter what happens, we won't blame you. I promise. We just want to play hockey."

"Yeah," Felipe said. "Ted's right. We have to play. *Please* ask your dad."

Junior was silent for a minute. "Okay," he finally whispered. "You asked for it."

We dragged him over to his dad's Jeep. Mr. Shrump was talking to Coach B.

"Dad," Junior said. "You don't want to sponsor the North Stars, do you?"

"Sponsor the North Stars? What an excellent idea!" Mr. Shrump boomed. "In fact, I was just asking Coach Baxter how your search was going."

"That would be great!" Felipe grabbed Mr. Shrump's hand and started shaking it. "Thank you. Thank you. Thank you!"

Mr. Shrump laughed super loud. "You're welcome, guys. I just have one condition."

"Anything," Teddy said quickly. "We'll

do absolutely anything."

"You have to add one more player to the team." Mr. Shrump put his arm around his son. "Ronnie."

"No problem," Coach B. said. "I think we already feel like Ronald is part of the No Stars. He's the best unofficial manager we've ever had."

"Well, you'll have to find a new unofficial manager," Mr. Shrump announced. "Ronnie won't have time for that now that he'll be playing for the team."

Junior stood right next to me. "Oh, no," I heard him groan.

"What's wrong?" I asked.

"Mike, you have *got* to help me," he whispered. "You can't imagine what a bad idea this is!"

But before Junior or Coach B. could say anything else, Mr. Shrump started bellowing again.

"Well, gang, I've got to go now, but I just want to say two things. First, I don't want anyone to call *my* team the No Stars. You're the *North Stars!* Shrump's—"

"Wait a minute," Junior interrupted his father. "I can't play for the North Stars. I don't have any equipment. All I've got is my old pair of skates."

"Huh?" Mr. Shrump said. "You know, Ronnie, you're right. Well, I can take care of that easily enough. Let's go to the Hockey Hut right now. I'll buy you everything you need."

"Great," Junior muttered.

Mr. Shrump boomed right on. "And you know what else I'm going to do? I'm going to order new jerseys for the whole team while we're over there. I'll even pay extra for a rush job so you can have them by the next practice."

"New jerseys!" I cried. "They're really

expensive. I figured we would have to finish the season in our old ones."

"I want to say one more thing," Mr. Shrump continued. "I've always dreamed of seeing my son out there on the ice playing hockey like his dad. This is going to be fantastic!"

Mr. Shrump slid behind the wheel of his Jeep. "Come on, Ronnie. Let's go shopping." Ronald slowly got inside, and they sped off.

"What kind of business does Mr. Shrump own?" Sari asked me.

"I don't know," I answered. Felipe and Teddy shook their heads.

"Well, I guess it doesn't matter. At least we have a sponsor," she said.

"Let's hope the Board of Health doesn't close it down," Felipe joked.

"It can't be worse than Spiro's Grease Trap," I replied.

Little did I know then how wrong I was. Things were going to get worse. Much worse.

From Grease to Grime

5

Junior was late for practice the next day.

"I bet he chickened out," I said to Sari. We skated around the rink, passing a puck back and forth.

"No, he's coming," Sari said firmly. "Mr. Shrump was on the phone with my mom about six times last night. She says he has a million suggestions to make the No Stars better."

"Let me guess," I said. "Putting Junior on the first line was one of his suggestions."

"Actually, you're close," Sari said with a frown. "He kept telling Mom that Junior is a natural center—Wow! Look at that!"

Sari pointed over to the bench. Mr. Shrump and Junior had just walked into the rink. Junior was decked out from head to toe in brand-new hockey gear. New shorts, new gloves, new helmet, new practice jersey, and just-out-of-the-box brand-new skates.

"Wow, he's wearing Royal Canadian 7000 skates," I said to Sari. We skated closer for a better look. "They're the most expensive skates around. I thought only the pros could afford them."

Mr. Shrump stepped out onto the ice. He was wearing a pair of Royal Canadian 7000s too.

"Hi, gang!" Mr. Shrump yelled to us. He sounded even louder in the big ice rink.

"Hi, Mr. Shrump," we answered.

We watched Junior step slowly onto the

ice. He didn't say anything. He just stood next to his dad with a sick look on his face.

"Hi, Ron," Coach B. said to him. "We're getting ready to start. Take a couple of laps around the rink to loosen up. Your dad can watch from over there." Coach B. pointed to the bleachers next to the bench.

"Go get 'em, Ronnie," Mr. Shrump boomed. He gave Junior a big slap on the back and then skated over to the bleachers. Mr. Shrump was a real good skater, graceful and natural.

As soon as Junior started skating around the rink, I knew why he looked so sick. He was terrible. I know some kids say they have trouble skating because they have weak ankles. But Junior must have had a weak body or something. He looked as if he were wobbling from head to toe.

Nothing went right for Junior during

practice. He missed easy passes. He fell down a lot. Once, when he took a shot, he missed the puck completely. The stick flew out of his hands and sailed across the rink. It just missed spearing Wayne, who dived for cover.

"Wow," I said to Teddy and Cliff. "I thought he would be a lot better."

"Yeah, me too," Teddy answered.

"You know, he's not *that* bad," Cliff said. "I fall down as much as he does. And Junior is still a better skater than Wayne. When you think about it, he fits right in with the No Stars."

"Come on, Ronnie! Wake up!" Mr. Shrump yelled. He sat way up at the top of the bleachers. But his voice was so loud, it sounded as if he were standing next to us.

Wayne handed Junior his stick. Junior skated over to us.

"Relax," I said. "You'll get better."

"You've got to get me out of this, Mike!"

he said fiercely. "I hate skating! My dad's been teaching me for five years, and I still can't do it."

"But you like hockey, right?" I asked.

"Sure, I like to *watch* hockey. I like being on the bench and helping you guys. But I don't want to be out on the ice."

"Why don't you tell your dad?" Teddy asked.

"He knows how I feel," Junior said miserably. "We argue about it all the time. He keeps telling me that I should try playing, that then I'd like it."

"Maybe he's right," Cliff said. "I never played before this year. When we lived in Arizona, I never saw a hockey game. I thought all skates had wheels on the bottom of them."

"Yeah," I said. "Cliff thought ice was something you put in your soda!"

Cliff laughed. "That's right. So when Mike told me I should join the No Stars, I thought he was crazy. But once I tried it, I really liked it a lot."

"It's different with me, Cliff," Junior said. "I already know I don't like skating. This is my dad's way of forcing me to play on a hockey team. Just like he did."

"Look," I said. "Maybe there's an easy way out. You could wear the uniform and just sit on the bench the entire game."

"That will never work," Junior assured me. "My dad wants me to *play*. Not sit on a bench."

"But your dad won't be here all the time, will he?" I pointed out. "He has to go to work. If he's not here watching, you might like playing."

"I told you, Mike. My dad is nuts about hockey. He's going to be at *every* game *and* practice for the rest of the year. He'll be here *all* the time," Junior insisted.

"Just stand there," I told him. I skated about ten feet away. "Now I'm going to pass you this puck. All you have to do is hit it back nice and easy."

I hit a soft, slow pass to him. Junior stopped it with the blade of his stick. His pass back to me was pretty good.

"That's the way," I said. "Let's do a couple more, then I'll move farther away. You just need some one-on-one practice."

"Thanks, Mike," Junior said. "But you're wasting your time."

A couple of minutes later, Coach B. blew her whistle. "Come over here, gang!" she yelled. "Our new jerseys have just arrived!"

"Awesome!" Teddy said to Junior. "Your dad got the Hockey Hut to make up new shirts in one day!"

I spotted two cardboard boxes on the bench. Mr. Shrump stood next to them with a big smile on his face. We all hurried over to the bench. Except Junior. He stayed out on the ice.

Mr. Shrump opened up one of the boxes and pulled out a white jersey. It had RYAN spelled across the back of the shoulders in black. Right above the number 99 in purple.

"This is yours, Gretzky," Mr. Shrump yelled as he tossed the jersey to Teddy.

"Thanks, Mr. Shrump!" Teddy said. Wayne Gretzky is his hero. Teddy has always wanted to wear Gretzky's number, 99.

"Here's yours, Felipe. Catch, Sari, here's yours. Wild Man, you wanted 00—here it is. Mike, number 11—just like Mark Messier, right?"

Mr. Shrump tossed the jerseys to us as fast as he could pull them out of the box.

"And here's number 7—for R. Shrump, Jr.," he yelled. "Where are you, Ronnie?"

"Over here," Junior said quietly.

His dad threw the jersey to Junior. Junior didn't even try to catch it. It landed a few feet in front of him on the ice. I skated over and picked up the shirt.

That's when I saw the front of our new jerseys for the first time. I couldn't believe my eyes!

"Teddy, look!" I yelled in horror.

Across the front of our shirts were the words SHRUMP'S SEWER CLEANING NORTH STARS. And, for some reason, the uniform company had put "Sewer" and "Stars" in gold letters and everything else in purple.

"No way," Teddy said. "It looks like we play for the..."

"Sewer Stars!" Cliff cried.

"This must be some kind of trick," Felipe told Sari.

"I guess we now know what kind of business Ron's dad owns," I joked.

"He warned us," Teddy pointed out.

"Okay, gang, listen up," Mr. Shrump yelled. "I have a *fantastic idea*. To show your team spirit, everyone has to wear the new jerseys to school on Monday!"

For the first time in the history of the No Stars, none of us could think of anything to say. We stood there staring at the front of our jerseys.

"This is just great," I said. "Things are definitely going down the toilet."

Most of the time, I don't mind going to school. Felipe, Cliff, Sari, and I are all in the fourth grade at the Vince Lombardi School. So are a couple of the other No Stars. It's fun having so many hockey friends in my grade.

But Monday morning, I wished I could stay home. I knew that by the time I got to school, everyone would know about those stupid "Sewer Stars" jerseys. I thought about pretending I had the flu, but I knew I had no choice. We were a team. I had to go to school and stand by my teammates during the most horrible day ever.

The noise started as soon as I walked into school. Rick Gates, who plays goalie for the Penguins, was standing right by the front door. He made a sound like a flushing toilet.

"Ohhh, here's one of the Sewer Stars now," Rick said to Tony Kelley. Tony is the Penguins' captain. The Penguins are one of the best teams in town. Last year they won the Mayor's Cup.

"Hey, Beagleman," Tony called. "Congratulations. What a *great* name for your loser team."

I wanted to say something sarcastic, but I couldn't think of anything. I kept walking toward my locker.

I turned the corner and spotted Felipe and Cliff standing in the middle of the hall. They were staring at a big sign on the bathroom door. It said, PROPERTY OF THE SEWER STARS.

"This is worse than I thought it would be," Cliff complained.

"Stand back, guys. Here comes Lucas," Felipe warned us. Lucas has the worst temper of anyone on the No Stars. He gets called for more penalties on the ice than all of us put together.

Lucas had thrown his "Sewer Stars" jersey in the garbage can after practice on Saturday. But Felipe had made him take it out and promise to wear it. I smiled when I saw him today. Lucas was wearing his jersey—but it was inside out!

"What are you guys looking at?" he asked us.

We moved so he could see the sign on the bathroom door.

"Let me fix that," Lucas said. He pulled the sign down and stuffed it into a trash can.

"I think that door looks *much* better now," he said with a big smile. Then he walked down the hall, whistling to himself.

I had my first brilliant idea when I reached my locker. I would wear my parka all day. That way, no one would see the new jersey.

I hurried into Mrs. Nagan's classroom and sat down at my desk. I pulled out my history book and started reading it.

"Mike, haven't you forgotten something?" Mrs. Nagan asked me.

"No. I don't think so," I answered.

"Your coat, Michael. You still have your coat on."

"Well…uh…I think it's a little bit cold in here today. I thought I would just keep it on for a while," I explained.

"Come on, Michael. Hang up your coat," she ordered. "Now."

I knew I was beat. I headed for my locker.

When I came back to the room, I spotted a piece of paper on my chair. I picked it up and read it. It said, FLUSH AFTER USING.

I glanced around. Rick Gates sits two desks away from me. He grinned at me. I knew he was the one.

"Nice shirt, Beagleman," he whispered.

The rest of the day was a nightmare. Toilet jokes. Sewer jokes.

"That was the longest day in my whole life," I said to Lucas when we walked out of school.

"Me too," Lucas said. "Are you sure this is the only way we can still play hockey?"

"Yeah," I answered. "We have to have a sponsor. So we're stuck with these uniforms for the rest of the year."

"It's all Junior's fault," Lucas said.

"Wait a minute. He didn't want us to ask his dad to sponsor us, remember? We forced him," I reminded Lucas.

"So what?"

"Junior knew that if his dad was our

sponsor, we would have to wear jerseys with 'Shrump's Sewer Cleaning' on them."

"I guess you're right. At least he tried to warn us," Lucas said. "You know, except for talking too much, Junior is okay. I like having a manager. I lost one of my skates the other day, and he found it."

"Yeah, Cliff is always losing his mouth guard," I added. "And Junior keeps an extra one in the equipment bag."

"Too bad he can't be our manager," Lucas said. "But I guess his dad wants him to be a hockey star, like he was."

We walked all the way to my house before Lucas said anything else. "Do you think we'll get used to being called 'the Sewer Stars'?"

"We got used to 'the No Stars,'" I said.

"This is different," Lucas pointed out. "We're talking toilets here!"

"It's going to be a long season," I agreed. "Very long."

* * *

Our game that night was against the Flyers. At the warm-ups before the game,
Junior looked worse than ever. He could
hardly skate.

And the rest of us weren't much better.
Our drills were sloppy. No one paid atten-
tion to Coach B.'s directions. Finally, she
called us off the ice and led us into the
locker room.

Junior sat down between Lucas and me.

"Are you okay?" I asked.

"No," he said miserably. "I hate this. I'm
no good, and everyone knows it. It's like
this horrible dream and I can't wake up!
I'm going to quit!"

"Hold on a minute," I said quickly.
"Don't get carried away. Quitting would be
a big mistake. Just ask Lucas. He quit
once, and he's sorry he did. Right, Luke?"

"Yeah, that's true," Lucas said. "But I
have an idea that might make things better."

Lucas leaned over and whispered something in Junior's ear. After a minute, a big smile crossed Junior's face.

"Okay," he said. "I'll try that."

"Try what?" I asked.

Before Lucas or Junior could answer me, Coach B. blew her whistle.

"I don't know what's going on, but you guys have got to wake up!" she said sternly. "I heard about all the bad jokes at school today. Just forget about them. We're here to play hockey. So let's play! I've decided to change the first line. Ronald, you'll go in for Tommy. Give it your best shot, and don't worry, you'll do fine."

Coach B. started out the door and then stopped.

"One more thing. We don't have Ronald helping us *off* the ice anymore. So, Mike and Brendan, would you bring the water jugs out? Teddy, grab the towels. Sari, you carry the equipment bag."

We hauled everything out to the bench. Just as we finished setting up, the buzzer that starts the game went off.

An amazing thing happened then. Junior skated out in his jersey—number 7—and played great! I couldn't believe it. He skated with long, powerful strides. Just like his dad.

Then Brendan set him up with a smooth pass. Junior blasted it at the Flyers' goal. It bounced off the pipe with a loud *clang*. What a change! Junior looked like a star.

His dad was sitting up at the top of the bleachers. He was going nuts—yelling and cheering for Ron.

"Okay, Ronnie," he yelled. "That's the way. Take another shot. That one just missed."

The first period flew by. Junior kept up with the fast pace of the game, and took a few more great shots on the Flyers' goalie. But then, just before the end of the period, one of their best players, David Josephs, stole the puck and took off down the ice. Junior stopped in a spray of ice, turned, and skated after David.

Halfway down the ice, Junior stretched out his stick and tried to knock the puck away from David.

David lost his balance. He grabbed Junior before he fell. Junior's helmet flew off and bounced high in the air. David and Junior crashed to the ice. The buzzer went off, and the period was over.

I jumped up and skated out onto the ice. I wanted to make sure that Junior was okay.

Then I saw blond hair.

And I figured out Lucas's great plan.

Number 7 wasn't Ronald Shrump, Jr.

It was Lucas!

Good-bye, Mr. Shrump?

7

"**L**ucas, get over here. Right now!" Coach B. ordered.

"What's going on?" Mr. Shrump rushed down from his seat at the top of the bleachers. "Where's Ronnie?" he asked.

"That's what I'm going to find out," Coach B. answered. Lucas stood up and skated over to the bench. He had a big smile on his face.

"You want me, Coach?" he asked.

"I want an explanation. Why are you wearing Ronald's number? And where is Ronald, anyhow?"

"Uh, well, it's like this, Coach," Lucas began. "I spilled something on my jersey. So Junior, I mean Ronald, loaned me his…"

"Lucas," Coach B. said sternly. "No stories. I'm serious. What's really going on?"

Lucas took a deep breath and glanced around. Mr. Shrump was heading toward the locker room.

"Coach, Junior does *not* want to play hockey. He wants to be our manager," Lucas explained. "Tonight, he told us he was going to quit the team."

"Really?" Coach B. asked.

"We all got worried that Mr. Shrump wouldn't sponsor us if Junior wasn't on the team," Lucas said. "I thought that maybe we could fool him. So I put on Junior's shirt, and he stayed in the locker room."

Mr. Shrump entered the locker room. A few seconds later, we heard a lot of shouting.

After a couple of minutes, Mr. Shrump came back out. "What's going on here?" he bellowed. "Now Ronnie says he doesn't like playing hockey! That's the craziest thing I've ever heard of! He never felt this way before." He looked around at us.

"I don't blame *you.*" Mr. Shrump pointed at Coach B. "But I have a feeling that maybe Ronnie didn't think he was wanted by some of the other players."

Mr. Shrump's voice was so loud! All the people in the stands, and all the Flyers' players, were staring at us.

"Calm down, please," Coach B. said to Mr. Shrump. "You're way off base."

"I don't care," Mr. Shrump snapped. "If Ronnie doesn't play hockey, I'm not sponsoring the team!"

No More Toilet Troubles!

8

"**W**ait a minute, Mr. Shrump. Please!" Felipe called. "We'll talk to Ronald. We can make him change his mind. I'm sure of it."

Mr. Shrump gazed at all of us standing there in our Shrump's Sewer Cleaning North Stars jerseys. "Okay," he said finally. "Give it a try. Talk some sense into Ronnie."

"Okay, Mike," Felipe said to me. "You heard what the man said. Go in there and talk some sense into *Ronnie!*"

"Me? Why me?" I asked.

"Uh—because I'm the captain and I chose you," Felipe said firmly. "Go get him."

I slipped on my skate guards and walked down the hall to the locker room. After a few seconds, I realized that Teddy and Sari were right behind me.

"Why are you guys following me?" I asked.

"Maybe I can help," Teddy said. "Anyhow, I don't want to wait around and not know what's going on." His dark eyes blinked nervously.

"Me too," Sari said. "I have to know what's happening."

Junior sat on the bench in the locker room. He had already taken off his skates and put his sneakers on.

"Hey, guys," he said when he saw us. "Why are you looking so upset?"

"Because if you don't come out and play with us, your dad isn't going to sponsor the No Stars," I said. "And then we can't play at all. You've got to change your mind."

Junior shook his head. "No way, Mike. How many times do I have to tell you? I hate *playing* hockey! Anyhow, my dad's just bluffing."

"I don't think he is," I said.

"He'll calm down," Junior said. He pulled off one of his pads and threw it into his equipment bag. "And even if he doesn't, you'll find another sponsor. You don't need Shrump's Sewer Cleaning."

"Listen, Ron—" I started to say.

"Save your breath, Mike," Junior interrupted. He threw his other pads into his equipment bag. "I have officially retired from playing hockey. I'm out of here!"

Junior started zipping up his parka. I knew he would never change his mind.

"Junior," Sari pleaded. "You cannot quit! We need you too much."

Junior rolled his eyes. "Give me a break, Sari. I'm the worst player this team ever had!"

"We don't need you to *play* for us. We need you on the bench! You're the only person who knows where things are when we need them. Like the black tape for our stick blades. Or Cliff's mouth guard when he loses it," Sari said to him. "I bet you find Wayne's lucky water bottle three times every practice."

"That's right," Teddy said.

"My mom says that if you didn't chase us out on the ice, we would never get practice started," Sari continued.

"That's right," Wayne chimed in, opening the locker room door. "You're the best manager in the whole league." Wayne and Cliff sat on the bench next to Junior.

Junior turned bright pink. "Do you really think so?" he asked.

"We're not kidding," Teddy said.

"You've got to stay—as our manager."

"Do it, Junior," Cliff said. "Even if we find a new sponsor, we'll still need you. You really help us play better. So what if all your stats make me dizzy sometimes! I bet Coach B. would make you official No Stars Manager…"

Junior held up his hand for quiet. The five of us stopped talking. "Okay, okay. You talked me into it, guys," he said. "On one condition. No more calling me 'Junior.' My friends call me Ron." He looked at me. "Are you my friends?"

I nodded. "You bet. It's Ron from now on," I said.

"I'll make it official," Sari said. She pulled a black marker out of the equipment bag and wrote MANAGER across the front of Ron's jersey.

"That will do until we can get a team jacket for you," she said. "Just like my mom's."

That's when Coach B. walked into the locker room. She took a quick look at Ron's jersey and broke into a big smile.

"I guess this means I've got my manager back," she said.

Ron nodded happily. Cliff and Teddy gave him high-fives.

"Okay, back out on the ice. Let's go!" Coach B. said.

"Junior—I mean, Ron—what about your dad? Do you think he will still sponsor us?" Sari asked.

"I don't know," Ron said. "Let's go find out."

Ron led us out of the locker room. Mr. Shrump was waiting for us down by the rink. He didn't look very happy.

"You guys wait here," Ron said. "I have to talk to my father by myself."

Ron walked over to Mr. Shrump. They both started talking at once. I couldn't make out what they were saying, but it didn't look very good to me.

Ron was pointing out at the ice and shaking his head. Then he pointed over at us.

Then Mr. Shrump shook his head. Ronald said something else and pointed to his chest.

"What do you mean, the jerseys are no good?" Mr. Shrump boomed. "What's wrong with them?"

Ron said something I couldn't hear.

"They called you guys *what?*" he said.

Ron started to say something. But his dad cut him off. "Maybe sponsoring this team was a mistake."

"Mike, Mike!" Wayne said desperately. "Do something! Say something! Save Ronald! Save the No Stars!"

I turned to Felipe and Lucas.

"It's only a name," I said. "We've been called a lot worse than the Sewer Stars."

"I don't think so," Lucas said. Then he

thought for a second. "Well, maybe we have…"

"It doesn't matter," Felipe cut in. "We just want to play hockey. Somehow." He gave me a little shove toward the Shrumps.

I walked over to Ron and his dad.

"Excuse me, Mr. Shrump," I said.

"Not now, Mike. I don't want to hear anything else," Mr. Shrump said quietly. He was staring at Ron.

"Please," I begged him. "Just listen to me for a second. Don't be mad at Ron. He's a super manager. Before he came, we used to waste half of every practice finding all our stuff and getting organized. He does all that. So now Coach B. has more time to work with us. He's the most valuable team member."

Mr. Shrump looked back and forth from me to Ron.

"Do you *really* like being the manager?" he finally asked Ron.

"I love it!" Ron said. "I get to be on the team and hang out with the guys. And I don't have to skate! It's a great deal."

"It's true, Mr. Shrump," I said. "And one more thing." I took a deep breath as Mr. Shrump turned to watch the Flyers skate in circles on the ice. "The jerseys are great. We love them."

Mr. Shrump whirled around. *"What?"* He shook his head and then smiled. "You guys must really want to play hockey. Ronnie, you better get your team out there before the Flyers get tired of waiting and go home."

"All right!," I shouted. "He's going to sponsor us! He's going to sponsor us!"

A huge cheer went up from the rest of the team.

I hurried over to the bench. Ron and his dad followed right behind me.

"I'm glad you decided to stay," Coach B. said. "Both of you." She reached out and shook Mr. Shrump's hand. "This means a lot to these kids. All of them."

The buzzer went off. The second period was about to start. Ron picked up his clipboard. "Okay. First line on the ice. Cliff and Felipe on defense. Wild Man to the goal!"

Then Mr. Shrump leaned over and whispered something in Ron's ear.

Ron waved his arms and yelled. "My dad says we're sending these jerseys back to the Hockey Hut after the game. They'll take 'Shrump's Sewer Cleaning' off the uniforms. No more sewers. From now on, we're just the North Stars." We all cheered again.

If this were a TV movie, the No Stars would have gone out and beaten the Flyers, and then carried Mr. Shrump off the ice on our shoulders.

But what really happened was that Cliff fell down a lot, Lucas lost his temper and got a penalty, and Wild Man lost his lucky water bottle and even Ron couldn't find it.

And as for the rest of us…well, we played like real No Stars.

We lost 5–2.

But Mr. Shrump took all of us out for pizza anyhow.

LEARNING TO FALL DOWN

Hockey's a physical sport. You've got to learn to take the bumps and bruises. And if you know the correct way to fall, you'll have a better chance of not getting hurt. So remember these four important rules:

1. Always wear a helmet! And I mean *always.*

2. Never put your arm out to break your fall. You'll break your arm instead.

3. If you get knocked off your feet or lose your balance, try to fall on your

knees. That's where your pads are.

4. If you're falling backward, tuck your chin into your chest and pull your shoulders forward. You don't want your head to snap back against the ice!

Practice falling on your own before the game. Then you'll be ready when you get checked, which will enable you to stay in the game and score more goals!

Sari's Hockey Tip

TAPE YOUR STICK

Taping your stick properly can help you play better. You'll "feel" the puck on the blade of your stick and have better control of your passes and shots.

Start about an inch from the "toe" of your stick. Wrap a single layer of tape in a spiral around the blade. Stop about an inch from the "heel." Be careful not to use too much. Too much tape makes the blade heavy and hard to use.

If you want extra control, wrap a wad of tape near the end of the handle. That can

TAPE YOUR STICK

Taping your stick properly can help you play better. You'll feel the puck on the blade of your stick and have better control of your passes and shots.

Start about an inch from the toe of your stick blade — the end that gets the puck. Wrap a layer of tape in a spiral around the blade. Stop about an inch from the "heel." Be careful not to use too much tape. Too much tape makes the blade heavy and hard to use.

If you want extra control, wrap a pad of tape near the end of the handle. That can keep the stick from slipping out of your hand in the middle of a game.

Ronald's Hockey Tip

FREEZE THE PUCK

Always freeze your puck before you play. Just put it in the freezer a few hours before the game. A frozen puck is faster and easier to handle. Warm pucks bounce!

However, when hockey players talk about "freezing" the puck, they usually mean something else. It's a way of stopping the action when the other team is threatening to score.

"Freezing" the puck means trapping it, keeping it away from the other players. Try

holding the puck against the boards with your skate. Use your body to protect it. Or if the goalie's watching, push the puck under one of his pads. *Be careful not to push too hard!*

When the referee sees that the action has been stopped, he'll call for a face-off. This will give you time to get set up and maybe get the puck away from your end of the ice and down into your opponent's territory.

Jim O'Connor is the author of many books for children. Recent titles include *Shadow Ball: The History of the Negro Leagues, Jackie Robinson and the Story of All-Black Baseball*, *The Ghost in Tent 19*, and *Slime Time*, all published by Random House.

Jim was raised in upstate New York, where he learned to ski and ice-skate at an early age. He never played organized hockey, but he enjoyed playing lots of "disorganized" hockey outdoors during the long, cold winters. Jim's other favorite sport is long-distance running. One of his greatest thrills was finishing the New York City Marathon.

Jim lives in New York City with his wife, Jane, and their sons, Robby and Teddy.

Hockey is hot—and the No Stars are the _coolest_ team around!

Skate in on all the action with:

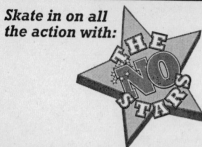

You can find more No Stars titles wherever books are sold...
_or_
You can send in this coupon (with check or money order) and have the books mailed directly to you!